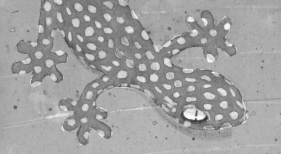

For my grandson, Emerson Bond,
who loves to climb. RH

For Mum. BL

First published in 2017
by Walker Books Australia Pty Ltd
Locked Bag 22, Newtown
NSW 2042 Australia
www.walkerbooks.com.au

National Library of Australia
Cataloguing-in-Publication entry:
Huber, Raymond, author.
Gecko / Raymond Huber; Brian Lovelock.
ISBN: 978 1 925126 55 6 (hardback)
Series: Nature storybooks.
For children.
Subjects: Geckos – Juvenile literature.
Other creators/contributors:
Lovelock, Brian, 1956– illustrator.
597.952

The illustrations for this book were created with
watercolour, acrylic ink and coloured pencil
Typeset in Chapparal Pro, Gararond and Journal
Printed and bound in China

10 9 8 7 6 5 4 3 2 1

The author is grateful for valuable advice from
Professor Aaron M Bauer, Villanova University, USA;
and Professor Alison Cree, University of Otago,
New Zealand.

Gecko

RAYMOND HUBER AND
BRIAN LOVELOCK

WALKER BOOKS
AND SUBSIDIARIES

LONDON • BOSTON • SYDNEY • AUCKLAND

Gecko peeks out of a crack in the cliff.
All clear.
He scurries down the cliff face and stops on a sunbaked ledge to warm up. There are many dangers in the daylight and Gecko is on high alert.

Geckos are "cold-blooded" and need the sun's heat to keep warm.
They must take care when out in the open because they have many predators. Geckos are eaten by snakes, birds, cats, rats, scorpions and large spiders.

Gecko cleans himself. He licks
the grit from his scaly skin.
Gecko's tongue whisks around
his face and wipes his eyeballs.
The sun will soon set and
Gecko is getting hungry – so
hungry he could eat his own skin!

Most geckos can't shut their eyes,
but see-through skin called a "spectacle"
protects the eye. Geckos have feet that
are self-cleaning so they don't need to
lick them.

Luckily, his skin is getting loose; it's the perfect time to peel. Gecko plucks and picks at his skin and squirms out of it. He peels his eyes too. And keeps them peeled for danger!

Gecko eats the crinkled skin – a snack off his own back.

As geckos grow, they shed an outer layer of dead skin several times a year. They eat the old skin so predators are not attracted by it.

Gecko beware!

A hawk is hunting. Time to disappear. Gecko's colour darkens and the fringe of his skin stretches out until his body seems to melt into the rock. The hawk wheels away and Gecko quickly seeks shelter.

Gecko camouflage includes: dappled skin patterns and colours; turning lighter or darker; and skin folds that flatten out so that the body casts no shadow.

13

He jumps onto a tree. What's this creeping towards him? A tasty cockroach! Gecko is as still as a stone until the bug is almost under his nose.

CRUNCH!

He strikes with strong jaws, and jerks his head back to swallow the cockroach whole.

Geckos eat insects, worms, fruit, and sometimes other smaller lizards. They have between 50 and 300 tiny teeth.

It's dark now and Gecko climbs
higher to search for flying food.
He weaves between leaves, slinks
along branches, trickles over twigs,
his tongue flicking out to smell the air.
　　Gecko dangles from a branch and
snatches a mosquito, the first of
many that night.

Most geckos are active at night.
They have big eyes so they can see
in the dark. Geckos smell with their
noses and tongues.

In the morning, Gecko finds a shady overhang where he can snooze for the day. He clings upside down on the smooth rock. But Gecko doesn't see the rat watching from the shadows.

Geckos' feet have a powerful grip thanks to toe-pads covered in "setae", which are like tiny hairs. The setae are branched into a billion spatula-like tips, which can hold on to any surface.

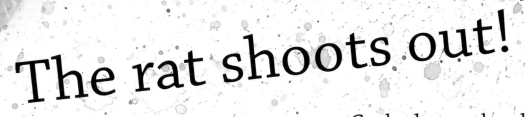

The rat shoots out!

Gecko hears the clip of claws just in time. He kicks off the rock and nosedives onto a ledge below.

Go, Gecko, go!

Geckos have excellent hearing. They are fast runners and nimble movers, having flexible backbones and tails that help them balance.

The rat leaps!

The rat lands on Gecko's tail, pinning him down. Gecko drops his tail, runs into a crevice and wedges himself in. Will his tail-trick fool the rat?

A gecko can break off all, or part of, its tail. The disconnected tail still squirms to distract or deceive a predator while the gecko escapes.

Gecko waits a while then pokes his head up. The rat has returned to its cave, but what's this? It's only eaten part of the tail. Gecko carries it back into the cranny and devours it.

A gecko will eat a dropped tail if the predator does not: it's full of fat, too good to waste. A new tail will grow within four months.

As night falls once more, Gecko skitters to the top of the cliff. His sharp eyes spy a flash of colour below – the freckled skin of another gecko. He must warn this intruder off his patch.

Geckos are one of the few animals in the world that can see colours at night.

Most male geckos won't allow other males in their area.

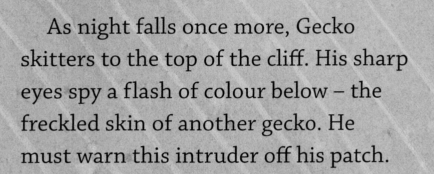

Gecko lifts his voice to the stars.

*Tok-tok-tok-tok,
gek-ko, gek-ko.*

The stranger scuttles away from the
cry. Gecko has defended his territory
and is safe once more.

Geckos are the most vocal of all reptiles
because they have a voice box. Their calls
are used to scare, to signal danger, or to
attract a mate. The name "gecko" probably
comes from the sounds they make.

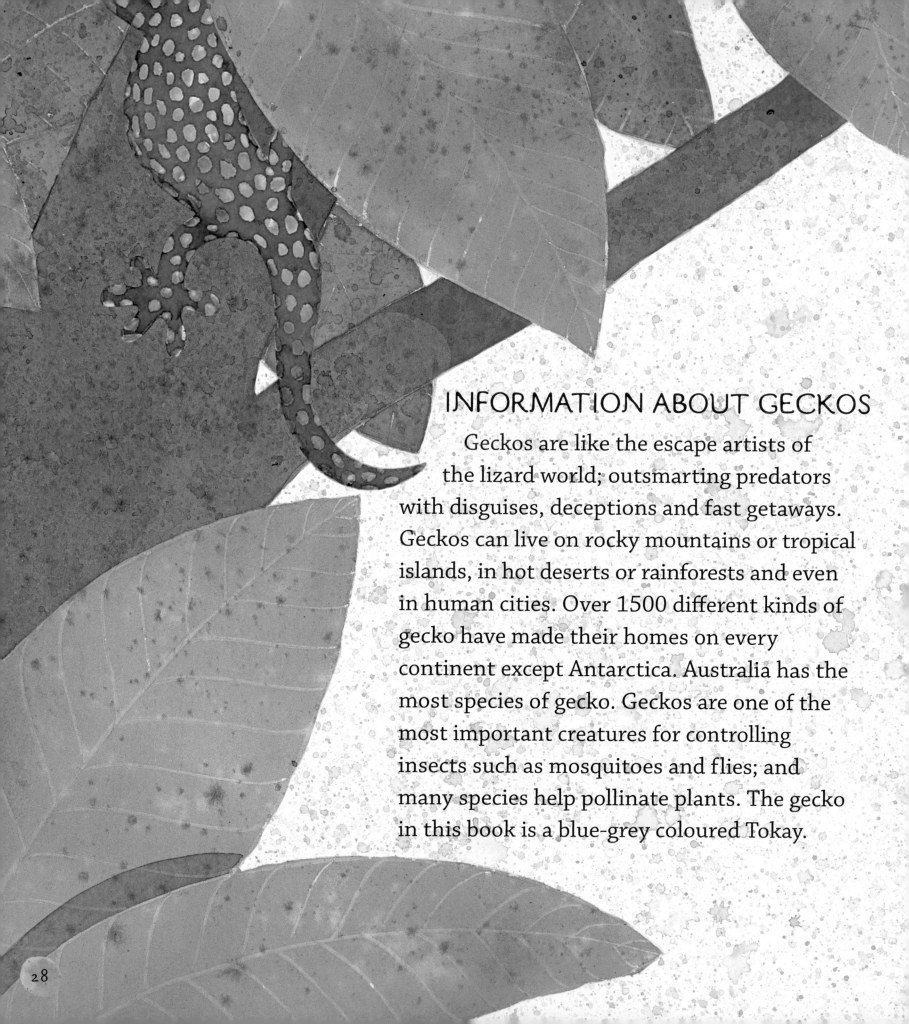

INFORMATION ABOUT GECKOS

Geckos are like the escape artists of the lizard world; outsmarting predators with disguises, deceptions and fast getaways. Geckos can live on rocky mountains or tropical islands, in hot deserts or rainforests and even in human cities. Over 1500 different kinds of gecko have made their homes on every continent except Antarctica. Australia has the most species of gecko. Geckos are one of the most important creatures for controlling insects such as mosquitoes and flies; and many species help pollinate plants. The gecko in this book is a blue-grey coloured Tokay.

INDEX

Look up the pages to find out all about gecko things.
Don't forget to look at both kinds of word –
this kind and this kind